Walk of Life

Walk of Life

The Poetry of Life and Experiences

LUIS BARRETO

Copyright 2020 © Luis Barreto.

All rights reserved. No part of this book may be reproduced in any form or by any electronic or mechanical means, including information storage and retrieval systems, without permission in writing from the publisher, except by reviewers, who may quote brief passages in a review.

ISBN: 978-1-63732-243-7   (Paperback Edition)
ISBN: 978-1-63732-244-4   (Hardcover Edition)
ISBN: 978-1-63732-242-0   (E-book Edition)

Some characters and events in this book are fictitious. Any similarity to real persons, living or dead, is coincidental and not intended by the author.

Book Ordering Information

Phone Number: 315 288-7939 ext. 1000 or 347-901-4920
Email: info@globalsummithouse.com
Global Summit House
www.globalsummithouse.com

Printed in the United States of America

A Walk Of Life
Dedicated to all my family members.
My wife Danielle Barreto
All those who believed in me

This is saying,

Thank you.

Contents

New Horizon..1

Wings of Gratitude 2

The Story Began..3

Running Towards Freedom 4

My Horizon 5

Make a Difference 6

Drift Me Away 7

Angered Soul 8

Bitter Cold 9

My Song to You 10

Why 11

My Coffee Life 12

How You Saved Me 13

What I do...14

What Do I Love About My Life...............................15

The Beat of Life 16

Economic Truth 17

My Poems 18

To The Next Level 19

My Cold Apology 20

Thankful..21

Two Worlds...22

Dream Car 23

Life's Problem 24

More Than Love 25

Romantic Desire 26

I Could Never Love Again 27

A Woman Alone in a Distant World 28

God is in Our Soul 29

Love has Arisen 30

Blue Moon 31

White Christmas 32

Purring Calico Cat. (Tiger Lily) 33

Sleepy Gray Tabby (Casanova) 34

Simply Meant To Be… 35

In my Prison 36

Zombie 37

Have Fun, Get Rich! 38

New Horizon

There is a beginning to everything in life, and it can be small or big. We may never know how it starts, but we do know that in the process we enjoy every minute of it. The first breath that we take can be our last, due to unfortunate events in our daily lives. The new horizon is a view past your dreams, while the reality of life seems hard we still have hope that we will overcome our troubles. Let us all unite and live the life we all desire, our goals are to view the New Horizon.

Wings of Gratitude

If I had wings I would soar far away and fast. At least that's what anyone would want to do. But, as for a poet such as myself, I would cherish life more than when I was wingless. Life has taught me to be grateful for everything and everyone. Live life to it's fullest and memorable moments.

The Story Began

The one day that has shaped everything that was total upside down in my life. It all began with a simple meet and greet and we decided upon ourselves to create memories. So far the first month has been extremely wonderful and filled with fun memories, that will last a lifetime. If I can't take you out to a fancy restaurant I can at least take you to a picnic or write my feelings for you in a poem. Whichever way, these are my feelings for you.

Running Towards Freedom

I don't want to lose you now, I 'm looking at the other half of me!" While running towards freedom, the finish line never seemed so far away and filled with so much horror. That we were forced to make split decisions whether to keep running or direct our helpless bodies to that other direction. The end is near, a finish line that is, and even though it is so close our minds are telling us to go the distance, despite the dangers that have surrounded us. In a great tragic state of mind, we as Americans are somehow accustomed to not fear what could hurt us. But fear what we didn't do at the exact moment when others needed our help. Ladies and gentlemen that is a fear no one could not bear to live with. Boston being a resilient city and standing strong it is in there nature, evil will have no choice but to fear the wrath of Bostonians. We will pray for them, fight for them, and stand united with them. You are weak, as your weakest chain, but untied we are strong and persistent, relentless, and fearless.

My Horizon

What I mean when I talk about a My Horizon? Hopefully, a new home, where laws are mandatory but fair. Where water is as pure as life itself. And it's readily available. Where most of us aren't watching others suffer and hear about their daily struggles. The end of poverty and rivalry. In reality, what has been taken from us, that makes us act in a disrespectful manner? I often ask myself...are we living right? Are some of us walking in the path of God? In which he paved for us to once follow righteously. These questions are asked frequently then they are answered nowadays. If these are the answers you seek, you will be searching for a lifetime.

Make a Difference

If I told you that I am writing to make a difference, in this cruel world would you believe that? Would you read it? I am writing this for the better word. For a stand that we should all take. Why settle? Why not better ourselves? It may sound similar to a priest, preaching to you but that's not me. I'm simply expressing my thoughts and emotions. On what I feel deep in my heart. With every fiber in my soul's heart. There are serious issues in this world that would not exist if we all are aware. This is the difference I would like to make.

Drift Me Away

Over the horizon, through the clouds in the sky, he would rather be in a state of relaxation. Feeling a sense of clarity while he is dealing with a world of troubles. The only world he is used to growing up has vanished from existence, no longer clinging to last memories or never-ending emotions. Forced to be resilient, life as he knew it has turned colder and bold. Though it is imperative he recovers from the tide of horror, the outcome is remarkable. Nothing short of success is unacceptable. On the move drifting away.

Angered Soul

If my beliefs were any greater than a usual person's beliefs my worlds would collide, making everything around me seem perfectly balanced. My life could be among the greatest it has ever been. Granted that I am blessed to be surrounded by those who have given their helping hand to me, somehow I managed to carry this burden. An angered soul that has brought nothing surprising, and everything that has led to this despair is due to my unbalanced soul. My torn unwritten life has gone into a whirl spin that has formed a massive dark cloud over me. How do I completely erase myself and return to the beginning? Start over to a more balanced world, a constructive surrounding that has not been torn. Maybe my world has been right this whole time, and my soul will find peace soon in time.

Bitter Cold

While I am feeling a cold deep feeling that is running through my veins then I must say I am feeling pretty much alive tonight. The deep cold emotions that you try so much to avoid, I have no choice but to feel like it is nothing new. Everything is new to you and to me it is second nature. My soul has departed my hardened body. Blood has turned into a frozen liquid that I no longer have my crystal heart pumping blood. A clear cut into my skin leaves not a scar but an imprint of how much suffer and agony I have encountered. The real results of my despair can be read through my dark eyes. Someday this will all change, and I will be led out of the cloudy tunnel. The glorious light will shine through and I will triumph.

My Song to You

You think my life is great, or even amazing right just because I have everything in life. Let me assure you that you are seriously mistaken. I am sure you do not know one good thing you just look at the negative of my hardship. The way you look at me tells me a lot about you, even if you tell me that it is nothing like I see it. Most peoples will blind you, and when that happens you will be vulnerable to the truth. Will you believe everything they sell you, or will you fight for the truth, even if it hurts. Do not close your eyes, even if your eyelids are heavy, sleep-deprived, or your feeling tired. I know I might sound harsh, because of what I am telling you. Is it right, for you to block me from your hearing, but you being blind to the fact, will catch up to you in the end. This is my truth, my song to you.

Why

Why must I suffer and hurt Lord? Is it because my life is not going right but wrong? I ask myself what have I done? I try to walk in your path like you have asked, and say my prayers before I fall asleep. No matter what I do or done in the past or present the pain still lingers inside me like a free demon. Staying positive is my main duty for example the Armed Forces are forced to serve and do tours away from their loved ones and how would you feel if that same person, says that they will come back, but you know that is not going to happen. Therefore, you live your life and everything surrounding you is an unstable lifestyle. You keep reminiscing, thinking, barely breathing, while looking at photos sooner or later you can barely look at it. Being far away, from the ordinary way of living, you start to talk to yourself. Asking the same question, while the pain never seems to end, it has no beginning, nor does it take a vacation. We must find ourselves and put an end to this whirlwind tornado. Life is a rodeo and we must ride the bull with force, never give up and never retreat. We were put on this earth to fight and to accept life, as wrong as it maybe we are blessed to breathe. Also our younger generation, we must lead by example and teach them about the wrong and right and how life can get. Do not let them forget about showing respect to their elders, and the small things to take it day by day. One day they will understand this very question. Why?

My Coffee Life

Whenever I had a bad day I would solve it with a hot cup of coffee. If it was a cold day hot chocolate would wash away all my problems. Although it's only for a temporary time, the results would be rewarding. My friends and family circle has also taken a huge toll on me explaining the facts of life. I still desire a cup of coffee to simplify and distract any arising occasion.

How You Saved Me

You've saved me in many different ways even when I was down under in my own prison. Incarcerated and against my own will. That's how I felt before you arrived with your cheerful smile and amazing personality. Maybe I am over-analyzing what is happening, but it is a dream and I do not want to be awakened because if I am it will not come true....

What I do

If I'm broken then you must think I'm a joke a minority, a guy with no priorities. I'm looking for a job but no one is hiring, you might think I am lying but I'm out there always trying and looking. Do you think I'm doing alright if I am then you just got lied to fool! Cause my misery is me being realistic and when I'm not smiling then I'm not eating and when I don't eat I'm starving. Call me the Grim reaper cause I'm in the darkness, like a recon sniper. My heart has faded from me, and when I open my heart it's an epidemic plague. No one cries for me, cause I want my family to smile and pray when I leave, my life has touched millions and I will continue to do that. This is what I do.

What Do I Love About My Life...

Expressing something about love that was in my life was the very same person that inspired me to write this poem. My life was complete without errors nor small mistakes, my day was brightened with the sensation of her love for me. I wanted is to right in her eyes, even though I was thousands of miles away from her touch. Though it may seem as we were an old married couple that has been together for decades. The truth is we have been separated, by turning tables. A blockade stands in the middle of our path. In which it stands very well guarded. She stands her own, with her brave heart fearless of anything that crosses her way. As for myself, my defense has weakened, the battle was lost but not over. My love will shine for you if lost look for the beacon in the sky and the light will guide you to me. If I was asked what do I love about my life, I'll recite this poem to the very person who inspired me to write this.

The Beat of Life

Not all the training and the anticipation could prepare your family and yourself for what's to come in your life. Time will pass along like a calm ocean waves, as well as the winds shifting direction from time to time. The moon will be your beacon showing you the direction to home. Whether it's a full or half-moon, whenever lost, and feel down because you think you are alone. Take a minute and realize that your not, and you never were. From the time you get up, till you fall fast asleep the tempo of your life does not change. Just your surrounding does but we as humans cannot change that. It is human nature, and we must become accustomed to the beat of life. Same as the beat in your heart, we live by that beat. From days to weeks to months the beat will become in sync as you get closer to your return home. Then you realize all that time you spent away has passed by you so quickly. The sooner you follow the beat the quicker you will be reunited with your loved ones. Therefore enjoy the beat of life and remember it is only a year, you will be home in no time.

Economic Truth

I know others who have taken time from their busy lifestyles and those who know me, have witnessed these hard times with me. As you read on and on you can probably tell that this poem will be all about what I have experienced until now. This is not one of those sappy, "My life will get better" type of poems. This is my truth on what I believe is happening and what I do not see happening. Let us take a second and think about how the economy used to be and how it was easier to afford almost anything we could want. When the war was over business was booming way back in the "Roaring Twenties" when industrial growth set in numerous states and countries. Right after the aftermath of World War I, the economy was rapidly growing, which became known as the "Golden Twenties." then all that glory and prosperity ended with the stock market crash that happens to occur in 1929. The reason I mention this is because situations like this cannot be controlled and whenever this happens we tend to believe that we are stuck and will never surface. We all know life goes on, and they will be expenses that will tempt us to spend more of our income than possible, but we clearly know that we are not in any position to give in to the system. Be honest, if we have it we will spend it then regret it later when we then needed that extra cash. Nevertheless, we must be honest with ourselves and accept that it is going to be up to us to change these difficult times and be wise of the choices we make that most of the time comes back to haunt us.

My Poems

My life, my body, and spirit. If I should ever fail you, please don't let me die in vain. Let me continue the fight till my last dying breath.

To The Next Level

Wonder what is the next step in life? Where do you go from one step to another? Don't worry, just take it to the next level.

My Cold Apology

My cold feelings have caused me to be someone I am not, someone who clearly was not the person who you fell for. I realized that my apologies are piling up and I know too well what happens when there are no feelings left for forgiveness. You suddenly become numb and immune, to the pain caused by that very person you thought you knew. These emotions can happen as fast as you can try to prevent them. I clearly do not blame you because after all you are human and you should not be going through this. Nevertheless, occurrences in life arise without notice or a simple warning. Almost if it was a natural disaster that happens before our eyes and when it is too late the damage has been done. All we can do from here on is pick up where we left off, and rebuild our empire. My wish is to predict when the next disaster is going to occur, and what we can do to prevent it at the same time, what would life be if we can always predict the future? Or if we lived day to day always knowing the next step of our lives? My best advice is to be prepared and be ready to stand up to the tide.

Thankful

Why do I live like this?
I am filled with fear and fright.
Why must my nights be filled with no lights, only darkness?
Why does the water flow so calmly and peacefully?
And why can't life be ever calm and free of hate?
Lord told me to be thankful for what I have.
But now I'm thankful for what I don't have.
I'm grateful for not being in the streets.
My mom wants me to live and to forgive,
But all I want is life.
This poem goes to the people who questioned themselves.
You're not alone,
Just hold on.
Amen.

Two Worlds

If I could choose two worlds,
I choose Heaven before Hell.
Hell, before the cell.
The cell after me dying.
And you better believe I'm trying to live this life right.
But it's hard when the Devil is by my side.
And the skies look gray, and rain falls every night.
The sun shines, but not in my place.
Over the skies, but not down on me
I see my shadow, but that's just the light reflecting.
But it's affecting me in the long run.
I have no chance of seeing the sun.
This world I live in is so dark, so wrong.
They are filled with hate.
I want to see the light shine over me.
To let me know, I still live.

Dream Car

One car, one road

One song.

I was driving along the dark road.

Thinking nothing can stop you.

You feel free and relaxed.

The music picks up.

Speed increases.

High acceleration.

Adrenaline rushes,

And you feel lifted about your true feelings.

Your emotions rise to the stars.

Above the blue moon

The night doesn't seem so dark with genuine emotions.

Light begins to shine above you,

And you reach your destination.

The night rush has to come to an end.

You rest,

And tomorrow is another adventure.

Life's Problem

Too many to deal
With one too many
To ever solve,
Once I get involved in the lives,
I turn to run away from it all.
I ask for guidance.
I get nothing.
One too many situations I had to face
The world looked like a lonely place.
For those with lonesome souls
That feels like me.
Here's help.
It all starts with a simple prayer.

More Than Love

How does it feel to be loved?
And the person you're with loves you too.
It feels like I'm starting over,
And the whole world is new.
My nights seem filled with a sparkle.
That's the only thing I need from life.
I'm no longer alone.
Before, I felt like a shadow cast in life.
A walking spirit.
Love seemed like a faraway dream.
Till one night, you changed everything.
You told me it was just a phase.

Romantic Desire

I am fulfilled by desire, love, and compassion.
It's what makes a genuine, long-lasting romantic relationship.
I am amazed by its power and wisdom.
It beholds upon the specific individuals.
Just like everybody pictured,
A wonderful life with one another
Loyalty takes place,
And so, with that being there.
Love begins to unfold.

I Could Never Love Again

For once, I will give up on love,
And all of its desires.
If it's meant to be,
Then we will love till the end.
Your love is unique
With a slight touch of salt
Bold and understanding.
You love everyone but me,
That's what hurts.
I would do anything in my being to make it just,
But without you,
I could never love again.

A Woman Alone in a Distant World

So far away,
Far from the distant world
There lies loneliness.
Far apart from ordinary life.
A single person,
Stuck in this forgotten world cries.
We are lost without hope ever to love.
What the lonely woman often wanted.
She was betrayed by love.
She is patiently waiting for the spark of what could be her only savior.
Through life, she learned to let go of all that doesn't matter.
Only her hope and faith have kept this woman alive.

God is in Our Soul

Poetry for the soul.
Through hard times,
Hatred has taken a toll on our soul.
We, society, can't become the breeder for hate.
Must overcome the cracked road
To realize that God is in our souls.
We are walking Angels with a purpose to live.
Learn from life experience,
To only be misled by anger.
To face life in a whole different manner.
Wisdom has kept informed on daily problems.
My mission is to live and await my time.

Love has Arisen

Every moment we look into each other's eyes,
I completely lose my focus.
Every kiss is filled with enormous passion.
Always need it.
Once broken,
Can't ever be replaced.
Morning comes.
Birds are chirping.
Sun is warming up a new day.
New start of the quest for love
Adventure is the keyword in our world.
Love has arisen.

Blue Moon

Outside the cold winter forest,
Along the boardwalk,
On the lonely beach
Through the dark streets of Venice
A stranger was looking for his loved ones.
Little did he know what had occurred during the cold night.
As the stranger walks down the sidewalk,
He comes across a newspaper explaining a tragic event.
The events of the blue moon
Details can only explain so much.
To know what the stranger was feeling.
Feeling lost,
Crying,
Anger,
The exact blue moon feeling.

White Christmas

Beautiful lights on the roof of the house
People in the hustle and bustle.
The reindeer display in the front yard
Songs played on the stations fill me with so much joy.
I was picking that perfect gift for the ones that I love.
I am always thinking of those that don't get to spend Christmas with loved ones.
For some, there is no Christmas.
With my loved ones around,
It will be a white Christmas for me.

Purring Calico Cat. (Tiger Lily)

Why do you purr as so?
Why you look out the window, what do you see?
You keep me company and remind me of what love is supposed to feel like.
You cannot stay in one place, you must wonder and explore.
Purring calico cat where did you go? Climb as far as you can go, meow as loud as a violin.
Purring calico cat loves me as I love you.

Sleepy Gray Tabby (Casanova)

You are nowhere to be found, but you always come around.
We hear your faint jingle and we know it's you.
Light steps, but a big heart, unlike any cat I've known.
You mean well when you want your space.
But you always hang out with us every day.
Sleep is a big part of your daily life, I wonder what you might do if you didn't sleep at night.
Would you wonder and explore?
If you could fly would you so?
Sleepy Gray Tabby we love you so.

Simply Meant To Be...

Who are we to be free when we aren't who we want to be?
Are we simply meant to be?
Be together forever, for better or worse.
Is the worse over or the beginning of a horrible nightmare?
Married into a life we did not choose but we have to cherish it.
Do we do better the second time around? Do we get a second chance at redoing this life?
All these unanswered questions that we choose to ignore. Life is good as we make it. We are simply meant to be.

In my Prison

I am a prisoner in my own designed prison.
Unable to escape or even manifest me into my better self.
I'm in jail that has no exits, no light, and no connection to the outside world.
Just a four-wall dome, that keeps getting smaller and smaller as I get older.
The older I get the loneliness keeps mounting up till I cannot feel anymore.
No emotions whatsoever will ever be a part of me.
This is my prison.

Zombie

I often feel and have accustomed myself to think like a zombie.
Every day of our daily lives has been similar and until we decide to change it
We will always be a zombie. Going on through our routines like it is ok to live this way.
What can we do differently to awake ourselves from this nightmare? Or is it a nightmare?
We carry a lot of burden from our past that we neglect what's in front of us. As for myself,
 I have risen from the ashes into a new person, and refuse to be a zombie.

Have Fun, Get Rich!

If you could have anything in the world, what would it be? Would it be fame? Or would it be fortune?

That is the million-dollar question that anyone would ponder. Life is full of glamor and less worry.

All the time to do what you were destined to do to just simply enjoy life's gifts. Everything stops for one wonderful moment.

A moment that is questionable for anyone with a brain, unlike a zombie who falls into the divine trap. While we sit back and ponder this unforgettable question. Ladies and gentlemen, Have Fun. Get Rich!